The Foolish Tortoise

The Foolish Tortoise

Pictures by Eric Carle

Written by Richard Buckley

LITTLE SIMON

New York London Toronto Sydney

A tortoise, tired of being slow,
Impatient to get up and go,

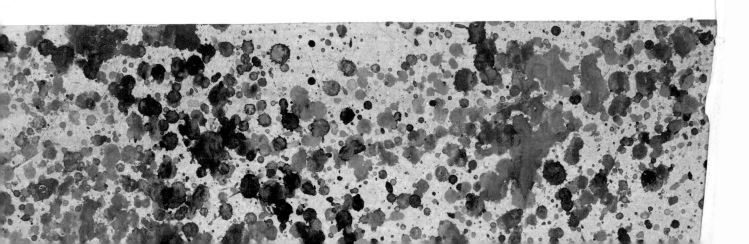

Took off his large and heavy shell
And left it lying where it fell.

"Hooray!" he cried. "Now I've been freed—
I'll see the world at double speed!"

Though faster, he was not express
And his protection was far less,
So when he heard a hornet's drone
The tortoise crept beneath a stone.

A hungry bird came swooping past,
He looked so fierce and flew so fast,
The tortoise hid behind some trees
And felt quite weak behind the knees.

"I don't feel safe, there's too much risk.
If only I could be more brisk!"
He headed for the riverbed:
A fish swam up, the tortoise fled.

Along his way our hero went
And almost had an accident.
A snake with open jaws slid near.
The tortoise backed away in fear.

A hare, a hound, a horse raced by—
So rapidly, they seemed to fly.
The tortoise gasped, sat goggle-eyed—
"I'll never be that quick," he sighed.

He wandered on, the sun rose high.
"I wish I had more shade!" he cried.
A sudden thunderstorm swept in,
And soaked the tortoise to the skin.

The wind rose up, and soon the breeze
Was bending branches in the trees.

The tortoise shivered. "Now I'm cold.
I wish I hadn't been so bold."

"I think I've lost the urge to roam,
I think it's time that I went home.
Without my shell I don't feel right."
So when his shell came into sight,

He climbed back in and said,
"Goodnight!"

 LITTLE SIMON

An imprint of Simon & Schuster Children's Publishing Division

New York   London   Toronto   Sydney

1230 Avenue of the Americas, New York, New York 10020

Text copyright © 1985 by Richard Buckley • Illustrations copyright © 1985 by Eric Carle

This Little Simon edition 2010. Originally published in 1985 by Picture Book Studio.

LITTLE SIMON is a registered trademark of Simon & Schuster, Inc., and associated colophon is a trademark
of Simon & Schuster, Inc. • For information about special discounts for bulk purchases, please contact
Simon & Schuster Special Sales at 1-866-506-1949 or business@simonandschuster.com. The Simon & Schuster
Speakers Bureau can bring authors to your live event. For more information or to book an event contact
the Simon & Schuster Speakers Bureau at 1-866-248-3049 or visit our website at www.simonspeakers.com.
Eric Carle's name and logotype are registered trademarks of Eric Carle.

For more information about Eric Carle and his books and products, please visit: eric-carle.com.

For information about The Eric Carle Museum of Picture Book Art, please visit: carlemuseum.org.

Manufactured in China 0910 SCP • 10 9 8 7 6 5 4 3 2 1 • ISBN 978-1-4424-2139-4

This special edition was printed for Kohl's Department Stores, Inc. (for distribution
on behalf of Kohl's Cares, LLC, its wholly owned subsidiary) by Simon & Schuster, Inc.
7-81375-21820-6 • Kohls • 14-421820-12 • 123386 • 09/10-02/11

Eric Carle was born in Syracuse, New York, and moved to Germany with his parents when he was six years old. He studied at the Academy of Graphic Arts in Stuttgart before returning to the United States, where he worked as a graphic designer for the *New York Times,* and later as art director for an international advertising agency. His first two books, *1,2,3 to the Zoo* and *The Very Hungry Caterpillar,* gained him immediate international recognition. The latter title, now considered a modern classic, has sold more than thirty million copies and has been translated into forty-eight languages. Eric Carle and his wife, Barbara, divide their time between the mountains of North Carolina and the Florida Keys.

Richard Buckley is a much-traveled English writer of both prose and poetry. He has lived in New York, Paris, and London, but his present home is in Cheltenham, England, where he has lived for the past thirty years, bringing up two sons with his Austrian wife (and muse) Elfie, a former Montessori teacher.